Sun's Diary

Telma Guimarães
Ilustrações: Rômolo

© Editora do Brasil S.A., 2016
Todos os direitos reservados
Texto © Telma Guimarães
Ilustrações © Rômolo

Direção geral: Vicente Tortamano Avanso
Direção adjunta: Maria Lúcia Kerr Cavalcante de Queiroz

Direção editorial: Cibele Mendes Curto Santos
Gerência editorial: Felipe Ramos Poletti
Supervisão de arte, editoração e produção digital: Adelaide Carolina Cerutti
Supervisão de controle de processos editoriais: Marta Dias Portero
Supervisão de direitos autorais: Marilisa Bertolone Mendes
Supervisão de revisão: Dora Helena Feres

Coordenação editorial: Gilsandro Vieira Sales
Assistência editorial: Paulo Fuzinelli
Auxílio editorial: Aline Sá Martins
Coordenação de arte: Maria Aparecida Alves
Design gráfico: Ana Matsusaki
Coordenação de revisão: Otacilio Palareti
Revisão: Flora Vaz Manzione
Coordenação de editoração eletrônica: Abdonildo José de Lima Santos
Editoração eletrônica: Ana Matsusaki
Coordenação de produção CPE: Leila P. Jungstedt
Controle de processos editoriais: Bruna Alves

Dados Internacionais de Catalogação na Publicação (CIP)
(Câmara Brasileira do Livro, SP, Brasil)

Guimarães, Telma
   Sun's diary/ Telma Guimarães; ilustrações Rômolo. –
São Paulo: Editora do Brasil, 2016.
    ISBN 978-85-10-06142-1
1. Ficção juvenil   2. Inglês   I. Rômolo.   II. Título.

16-04496   CDD-028.5

Índice para catálogo sistemático:
1. Ficção: Literatura juvenil   028.5

1ª edição / 1ª impressão, 2016
Impresso na Intergraf Indústria Gráfica Eireli

Rua Conselheiro Nébias, 887, São Paulo, SP, CEP: 01203-001
Fone: (11) 3226-0211 – Fax: (11) 3222-5583
www.editoradobrasil.com.br

To my brother Fábio Villaça Guimarães Filho,
my sister Diva Guimarães Alcalde,
and to my American brother and sister,
Eric and Karen Rochelle.

For the wonderful moments we shared.

January 1st
Saturday

HAPPY NEW YEAR'S DAY

Hi again, dear diary. It's Sun, back to you.

I hope we have a fine year, with a lot of cool surprises. Here is the list of what I expect for this year:

- To have wonderful teachers (yes, it is my dream!);
- to be able to wake up late every day (yes, I am a positive person!);
- to have a lot of friends and also a better brother.

That's all for now.

Sadly, someone laughed at my name again. Mom and I were at the market when the register heard Mom calling my name. She said to the other cashier, "Weird name, isn't it?"

"You can call me Sunny" I replied.

"Oh, sorry, young lady!" she blushed.

"Never mind. It happens every day!"

I was upset.

But it didn't last long. Mom bought some nice stuff and I survived.

Here's a pic of my family again. That includes Bacon and Coffee, of course. They haven't changed that much since last year. Look at them! Mom has a new hairdo. Dad has some white hair and Cosmo a worse humor. But I still love my family!

Dad, Mom, my brother, me, our pets Bacon and Coffee.

You know, diary, Bacon doesn't know he is a pig. He thinks he is a dog. Coffee has also an identity trouble. He behaves like a pig sometimes. What can we do for those adorable pets?

Cosmo, my brother, hasn't changed at all! He is my nightmare during night and day. You know, brothers are always a nightmare for their sisters. They try to ruin our lives, listen to our phone talks, borrow money, tell our secrets to our parents and blablabla.

Well, I have just taken a picture of him. I might need it someday. Look at this: he was trying to make a hairdo to impress his new girlfriend, Peaches. He is so silly, isn't he?

January 19th
Wednesday

I have a new best friend. Her name is Apple. She is Peaches' sister. We are in 6th grade, same class. We met each other at Mom's hairdresser. Ms. Spencer, the girls' mother, took Apple to Mom's to have a haircut. We started talking and found out we would go to the same class. Her mom is from Mexico, like mine. They are fond of weird names, like ours.

She offered me her bacon snacks and I refused them because I am vegetarian. I explained her that our vegetarian diet excludes meat.

"Wow! It sounds… sad!" she replied.

"We don't eat dead people" I said.

"Wow! This is nice! I will think about being a vegetarian, too. But can you eat this?" she showed me her snacks.

"Yes, sure. I can eat whatever I want. But I choose not to eat certain things."

She told me their parents aren't vegetarian like ours. They are "normal", I mean, they eat meat, chicken, salad, and other stuff.

Well, diary, sometimes I feel fed up with being a vegetarian. Vegetarian or not, we are friends!

February 2nd
Wednesday

GROUNDHOG DAY

Today is Groundhog Day. Remember last year, diary? It was cloudy when a groundhog left its burrow. The winter ended soon, as the legend tells. Two years ago it was sunny and the groundhog saw its shadow and went back to its burrow. The winter did continue for six more weeks!

I hope there are lots of clouds in the sky and the groundhog can't see its shadow. The winter will end soon and we will go to the beaches early!

I think groundhogs are so cute, aren't they?

Coffee doesn't like groundhogs at all. Neither does Bacon. They run after the poor animal, trying to catch it! It is kind of funny!

Latest news!

Winter will continue for six more weeks. Snow, snow, snow.

Groundhog Rhyme

Groundhog, Groundhog
Will you come out?
Yes Sir, Yes Sir
If the sun is not about
Groundhog, Groundhog
The sun is shining bright
Then I'll hop back in and curl up tight

I like this rhyme. We are used to saying it when the groundhog appears!

February 5th
Saturday

My friend Apple and I talked about a lot of things yesterday, including our family! She asked me what my father does for a living and I said he teaches Astrophysics at college.

"What does that mean?" she asked me.

"It means he is an astronomer" I said.

"That's cool! He knows everything about stars and planets? I bet you and your brother have these names because of his profession!"

"Yes, you are right. It was a coincidence meeting my mom Aura. Sometimes I think it was on purpose!" We laughed a lot.

I asked about her family too. I wanted to know how she felt being a twin raised by a mom who is firefighter.

"It's OK. Kind of different, I think."

She then told me that last week her mom saved four ducklings trapped in a storm drain by using a duck call ringtone. Her dad is a dentist, which is pretty normal.

"Do you like your name, Apple?" I asked her.

"No, I like my sister's name, Peaches" she answered.

"I wish I could be Mary, Ann, Sue, Barbara… They are beautiful names" I told Apple.

"I love your name, Sun! It is so… sunny!"

February 13th
Sunday

I must tell you a secret, diary. There is a boy who I really love. He is kind of cute. There is one I hate from the bottom of my heart. Can you keep this secret until the day I die? Hope so!

Boy I love	Boy I hate
♥ Ricky	✗ Adam Liang
♥ Ricky	✗ Adam Liang
♥ Ricky	✗ Adam Liang
♥ Ricky	✗ Adam Liang
♥ Ricky	✗ Adam Liang

They are in my Facebook. Ricky is the best. Ever.

We love Valentine's. It's a great day. We all expect to receive a card. It can be from our dad, our best friend, our teacher. Last year Samantha and Emily got one from the same boy. It was kind of funny. He wrote the same silly things to each of them. His name was Samuel.

We have prepared cards for our best friends and our parents. They are our sweethearts forever!

February 14th
Monday

Look at these cards.

They are all for Ricky. I don't like him anymore. I think I like Liang. Look at his card:

Isn't Liang cute? I think so.

Oh, that's my card for Liang. I made it for him. Oops. For Ricky. But Ricky has too many fans.

Can I tell you a secret, diary? I don't hate Adam Liang anymore.

February 20th
Sunday

LEFTOVERS. I hate them. VEGETARIAN LEFTOVERS. What do you think about that? Don't you want to come over and try it? You can have mine!

We have to open the fridge every Monday, take off everything and eat. Not altogether. Then the family stays in the kitchen and prepares these leftovers that turn out to be this delicious vegetarian LEFTOVER MENU.

What is in the fridge?
Some tofu, four eggs, cauliflower, cabbage, broccoli, carrots, more tofu, soy grains, soy cheese, one avocado, beans, noodles, two eggplants.

What is on the table?
Veggie antipasto, salad, egg flower soup, tofu soup, noodle soup, vegetables, fried rice with egg, vegetable enchilada, soy juice.

Well, it's not that bad. But I have to confess, I'm crazy about hamburgers.

February 21st
Monday

Today we commemorate the President's Day. It's a federal holiday. It's always on the third Monday of February. My school is closed today. That's why I love the President's Day!

However, I have to do a research about the theme.

These are the presidents I like most: Abraham Lincoln (he was the first president), George Washington, John Kennedy, and Barack Obama.

I like Abraham Lincoln because he prepared the way for the abolition of slavery. I think George Washington was very nice when he stood in favor of religious freedom. I also like Kennedy because he was very young when became president. And I like Barack Obama because he said "Yes, we can". I try to say that to myself every morning: "Yes, Sun, you can wake up early in the morning and go to school!" LOL!

National symbols of the United States

The American flag

Statue of Liberty

Uncle Sam

American bald eagle

Washington monument

Capitol building

Declaration of Independence

Liberty bell

I think I might be a president someday.

February 26th
Saturday

Lunch at Uncle George and Aunt Myra's.

I love having lunch at my uncle and aunt's house. The food is delicious.

Uncle George and Aunt Myra, Mom's sister, have one kid. His name is Iago and he is eleven. He is nuts. But I like him.

THE MENU IS ALWAYS GREAT. TAKE A LOOK.

Chicken fingers, tuna sandwich, chili, pasta and meatballs, real grated cheese, fruit juice, and strawberry ice cream.

They have wonderful food. My parents don't like it. They think it is not healthy. If I tell Mom what I had for lunch, she will be mad at me.

February 27th
Sunday

I ate too much. From her bedroom, Mom heard me rolling over my bed, with a bad stomachache. She came to me and asked what I had had for lunch at my relatives' house. I said nothing. I don't like to lie.

Mom asked me to open my mouth. She said she could feel a strong smell of meat.

I hate it when Mom has a Sherlock attitude towards my tongue. She went to her pharmacy box and came back with some pills. I felt much better then.

Sorry, Mom. I am not a hundred per cent vegetarian.

March 1st
Tuesday

Science project

Our group has a science project to do. It's about water waste. I have to add a car, trees, and some plastic animals to help our watershed project look more like the environment in which we live. Sometimes I like Science. Sometimes I don't. I don't like it when something goes wrong. The cow fell on the floor and it broke in three pieces. I had to glue the pieces together. The head wasn't in the right place, but I think my teacher won't notice. Hopefully not.

March 4th
Friday

I love my brother. He is the best brother ever! Guess what happened! I fell down and our whole Science project got ruined. I was going to school and looked at Ricky. I fell down and so did our project. It broke into two. I started crying. Cosmo was behind me and picked up the project and took it to his first class. He glued everything with his powerful glue and it was fine again.

Apple and Samantha started explaining our project. I explained the final part. Unluckily, my cow fell to pieces. Some of the students laughed. I laughed too.

My Science teacher said our project was OK. I don't like the word "OK". I prefer "nice", "cool", "fantastic".

The other projects were also OK. You are also OK, teacher!

March 26th
Saturday

I love going to Mom's beauty salon. Sometimes I help her with the hairdos. I'm a good helper.

There is an old lady who likes her hair blue. It's pretty funny and last time I laughed and Mom told me to be quiet.

Our great-grandmother came over yesterday. She also had her hair dyed blue. Cosmo was pretty upset. He also wanted to dye his hair.

Sometimes Cosmo is so funny. But only sometimes.

April 1st
Friday

Fool's Day

Dad woke us up earlier this morning.

"Hurry up! It is an emergency! There are Martians in our backyard" Dad and Mom cried loudly.

I jumped off my bed and ran to the backyard. But no Martians were there.

Cosmo, Bacon, and Coffee were staring at the backyard like me.

"Where are the Martians, Dad?" we all wanted to know.

"April Fool's day!" they started laughing.

I couldn't believe they played a trick on us!

Well, our revenge was in the fridge.

When they opened the fridge to grab some oranges, they were scared to death.

Look at this, diary... Isn't it perfect? We found a horrible man's picture on internet. We cut it and put in a glass jar.

April 4th
Monday

I have to do a project about Martin Luther King, Jr. Most of my friends will look at Google to copy and paste information. I am going to look at Google too, but I am going to write my project by myself.

My parents have his most famous speech hanging on the wall of their bedroom, so every time I have to do my homework I look at it and read it again. I can tell it even by heart! It's called "I have a dream". King says in his speech that he had a dream that those white and black children would one day walk hand in hand and that one day sons of former slaves and sons of former slave owners would be able to agree to live together.

He won the Nobel Peace Prize in 1964.

Look at some of my notes below.

Martin Luther King, Jr.

From 1950 to 1970 African-Americans suffered a lot. They were treated different because of the color of their skin. There were laws which required separate hotels, benches in the buses, restaurants and schools. Martin Luther King, Jr. was thirty-five years old when he got the Nobel Peace Prize. He gave all the money he got for the prize to the civil rights movement. I bet no one did the same.

April 24th
Sunday

EASTER

Every Easter is the same. Our parents think we are children. We have to go to the backyard and look for our chocolate eggs made of soybeans. We say we love them, but in fact we throw them away. We prefer our regular Easter eggs made of cocoa at our aunt and uncle's house.

While we look for our soybeans Easter eggs, Mom and Dad play silly games. They always ask us riddles and Easter knock-knocks.

Why is it easy for little bunny chicks to talk?
*Because talk is cheap.

Where does the Easter Bunny get his egg?
*From eggplants.

What comes at the end of Easter?
*The letter R.

What's a good way to catch the Easter Bunny?
*Make noises like a carrot.

- Knock-knock!
- Who's there?
- Heidi.
- Heidi who?
- Heidi the eggs around the house.

- Knock-knock!
- Who's there?
- Donna.
- Donna who?
- Donna want to decorate some eggs?

After that, we sit by the fireplace for baby stories about bunnies, Christian stories, fairy tales, and fables. This is not an ordinary family, remember.

Well, diary, it's a weird family, but it's mine. And I kind of like it! LOL

May 4th
Wednesday

I have a Geography problem. In my brain map, Argentina is in Central America.

"Oops, is Argentina near Guatemala? Is Argentina between Belize and Honduras? Maybe it's beside El Salvador and Nicaragua. Or after Costa Rica and Panama…"

Everybody laughed at the teacher's comments. But I doubt they know it.

Oh, diary, they do. I have to study harder. Luckily, Adam Liang is offering to study with me. He is going to come over to our house to study. Lucky me!

Afternoon.

Cosmo is so funny! LOL, just kidding. I hate him. He can't stop singing the song "Don't cry for me Argentina, I'm in South America". Emily and Vicky are here and they are laughing all the time.

I will never forget where Argentina is.

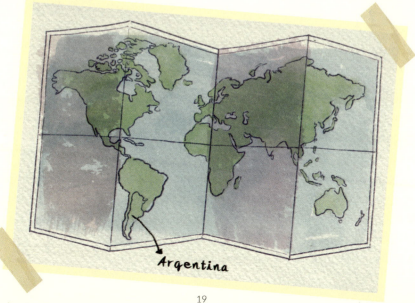

May 8th
Sunday

♥ MOTHER'S DAY ♥

Coffee wants to eat my homework. Bacon wants to eat my mom's present. Yes, it's Mother's Day. Dad says he is not going to buy Mom a present because she is not his mother. Cosmo is making a card. I am trying to make a lettuce cake. I know it sounds rotten, but our Science teacher says it's yummy. It takes apple, lettuce, and it is kind of healthy, I think.

After the cake and my brother's silly card, a little yoga in the backyard. Mom doesn't have a smiley face. Guess what! She was expecting a present from Dad. He tried to make it better with a gift card from a discount store.

Here it is:

"I couldn't think of anything else to give you... Happy Mother of My Kids' Day!"

May 21st
Saturday

I had a nice Geography test yesterday. Argentina is in South America now and Guatemala, Belize, Honduras, El Salvador, Nicaragua, Costa Rica, and Panama are in Central America, the way they were supposed to be.

Hanna, Sophia, and Vicky invited me to go to the movies. Three boys are going with us. I thought they were from 8th grade and took three hours and forty minutes to get dressed. But, diary, guess what? They were one of the girl's cousins, from 5th grade! Babies!

We met some guys in front of the movies: Ricky Cole, Adam Liang, and Bruno Myers. They were near some girls we don't like much.

I'm angry at the guys, mostly at Adam Liang! I hate him!

Late at night.

I don't hate Adam anymore. He left his friend (Rebbecca, the jerk one), bought popcorn and came to sit by my side. He tried to hold my hand, but it was busy holding the bucket of popcorn. I tried to hold his hand, but it was also busy grabbing the bottle of soda.

Cosmo and Peaches were sitting behind us. I could hear them kissing each other. They made a lot of noise. Apple, her sister, was sitting beside me and looked backwards all the time. She kept on saying, "I'll tell Mom and Dad, Peaches!"

I asked her not to tell her parents, otherwise my parents will punish my brother. And my brother Cosmo will tell ours that I sat beside Adam. You know, this is called "vicious circle".

May 30th
Monday

MEMORIAL DAY

Memorial Day is a United States federal holiday. It happens on the last Monday of May. It was first celebrated to remember the dead soldiers of the Civil War. After World War I, they decided to honor all Americans who have died in all wars. Memorial Day often marks the start of the summer vacation season, and Labor Day its end.

We woke up late. Dad wanted to take us to the cemetery and to the memorial. Mom didn't want to go with us. She stayed home to prepare a vegeterian barbecue. We sang our national anthem and made a prayer for the dead soldiers at the cemetery. When we came back home, we saw our USA flag on the pole in front of our house. We like to do that together, but I think Mom forgot it and did it by herself.

Uncle George, Aunt Myra, and Iago, my nuts cousin, came for the barbecue. Luckily, they brought meat. We were starving when we got home from the cemetery. Mom prepared grilled zucchini and baked some bread.

You know, diary, because Memorial Day is generally associated with the start of the summer season, it's common tradition to inaugurate the outdoor cooking season on Memorial Day with a barbecue. We had a normal one and a vegetarian one. You can choose.

June 8th
Wednesday

During our Art class, I decided to make a special T-shirt:

I did it because everytime I walk with Coffee and Bacon, people think we are a crazy family.

Everybody liked it and asked me to make one. Wow! Maybe I can open a store to sell a lot of pig T-shirts.

Look how cute Bacon was when he got home. I call these pictures "pigtures".

I know, diary, I agree. Coffee is jealous. I'll hand up his pic too.
He was Goldilocks last Halloween!

I love you both, Coffee and Bacon!

June 19th
Sunday

FATHER'S DAY

This is my report about Father's Day. I will present it to my English teacher on Monday. Hope she likes it.

> Father's Day in the United States is on the third Sunday of June. It was first celebrated on June 19, 1910 in Spokane, Washington, by a woman named Sonora Smart Dodd. She knew about Mother's Day and told her pastor she thought fathers should also have a holiday. She told him about her father, who raised six children by himself. The pastor thought it was a good idea. So the first Father's Day sermon was given on June 19, 1910.

I think I will give Dad a copy of my report. He might not know anything about Father's Day.

About the present: I decided to make crazy luggage tags. I know he is going to travel with Mom for a week, and I also know he lost his bag last year. It was hard to find it because it had no tags on it.

I hope he likes it!

June 29th
Wednesday

We laughed loudly during class this morning. Apple started it and Samantha and I joined her. We had no reason to do that. We just… laughed.

We were sent to Mr. Sanders' office. Mr. Sanders is our principal.

Apple and Samantha were as red as a tomato. So was I.

We felt very uncomfortable. Our Science teacher was mad at us. He asked us to stop, but we couldn't. It is not fair!

"Good behavior is something all parents and teachers expect… Your parents will like to see you studying. Concentrate, listen to your teachers, do your homework, and study for all tests! This is what you have to do at school. I will write a note to your parents."

And he gave us notes to give to our parents. I think we'll be in trouble!

> Your daughter was messing in Science class.
> She must behave better during class.
>
> Sincerely,
> *Jonathan Sanders*
> Principal

July 1st
Friday

My parents didn't like Mr. Sanders' letter.

"You are in trouble!" they said.

"What did you do during class?" asked Mom.

"We laughed. It was a silly thing Samantha told us. That was all."

"How do you feel now, Sunny?" asked Dad.

"I feel bad. We all make mistakes. But it was only a laugh. A loud laugh. Well, some laughs."

"We expect you to act better during class. Can you do that?" asked Mom.

"Yes, sure."

"We are going on a trip. You guys are going to stay at Uncle George and Aunt Myra's house. As soon as we come back from Mexico we will talk again about this, young lady!" they promised.

WOW! I am safe for now!

July 4th
Monday

INDEPENDENCE DAY

We woke up early in the morning. My uncle and aunt took us to the parade. We took our flags and tied our pets' handkerchiefs around their necks. There were lots of people at the parade. We saw the Veterans parade, the Marines, retired vets, the marching band. A huge flag was set in the middle of the main street while a choir of children sang the National Anthem. It was so cool! We had balloons and everyone let them go at the same time. The sky turned to be red, blue, and white.

INDEPEN...

We celebrate the 4th of July because it represents the day that America became separate from British rules. The colonists wrote a document saying they were no longer part of the British government. They also announced they were going to be a new nation called the United States of America.

This document is known as the Declaration of Independence.

On July 4th, 1776, the Declaration of Independence was signed, giving the United States independence from Great Britain. The Declaration of Independence was signed by fifty-six men representing the thirteen colonies.

July 5th
Tuesday

Wow, diary, Bacon and Coffee were at Uncle and Aunt's house with Cosmo and me. They hate fireworks and cried a lot.

This was my best Fourth of July. I'll tell you why.

After the parade, we went to our uncle's house and had "real" barbecue.

Coffee and Bacon had normal food too. We had lots of ice cream which tasted great with tons of fudge on top. Then we went to the market to pick up some movies to watch at home and met on our way Ricky Cole, Adam Liang, Peaches, and Apple. Aunt Myra let us invite them to come over her house. I was so glad and so were Cosmo and Iago, our cousin.

We had a lot of work with popcorn, more ice cream, more chocolate fudge. The movie was great, I think… Well, I'm not sure, we talked a lot during the movie… LOL.

Cosmo had a sort of fight with Ricky Cole because of Peaches. She was more interested in Ricky Cole. I think Ricky has a crush on her. Poor brother.

July 9th
Saturday

… We are still here! HELP!

My bedroom is a mess. My clothes stink, and so do Bacon and Coffee. I think I am going to fail 6th grade. I have a lot of homework to do, a report, a Geography project, and I must go to the library to pick up a book. I must read it until next Tuesday.

Can I tell you a secret? I MISS Mom's veggies, her colorful salad, I miss real food. Everything here is junk food. My hair smells like fried oil and so do my clothes.

I think I miss rules. They don't have any rules here.

My body itches. I saw some fleas!!! Probably Coffee's! He needs a bath!

I want to go back home!

July 11th
Monday

My pets are clean now. We bathed them. Coffee got rid of the fleas and so did I. No more sleeping together. I asked my aunt for some cream for fleas. Thank God I am not allergic to flea bites!

The book is on my desk. Can't write much. Must read it. Finished Science homework. Must do Geo project. Must do my laundry.

July 15th
Friday

Rescue DAY

Many things happened these days. Our lovely parents are back. Thank God.

I think Aunt Myra isn't Mom's sister. She's totally different from her. She is messy, eats too much junk food, doesn't clean the house and doesn't know how to raise children. Iago isn't polite, stays awake until midnight and goes to the bathroom with his mp5 player, tablet, and cell phone.

Luckily, holidays start today. Mom and Dad have to go to Mr. Sander's office and give him back that letter, signed.

I didn't do all my homework, my Geo project is awful and I didn't do well on the test about the book.

Can I put the blame on my relatives? Hope so!

July 26th
Tuesday

Mom allowed me to invite Apple to sleep over. Apple is here. We are watching a terrifying movie.

1 p.m.

We decided to phone up our crushes. I called up Adam Liang. It was 1 a.m. He was also awake. He was watching the same movie we were! LOL

Apple called her friend Trip. Don't ask me why Trip is his nickname. Trip was sleeping. His dad answered the phone and got mad at Apple. He asked:

"Who is there?"

"It's Sun. I'll talk to him tomorrow. Sorry, Mr. Hill."

I couldn't believe Apple said MY NAME instead of hers.

1:25 p.m.

We are in the kitchen making a sandwich. Sandwich bread, cheese, tomato, pickles, ketchup, mustard, peanut butter, strawberry jam. Weird, isn't it?

2:27 p.m.

Starving. I found some slices of zucchini and mozzarella cheese pizza in the freezer. WOW!

July 27th
Wednesday

I spent the whole day at the hospital.

I was feeling so bad!

The nurse: What did you eat yesterday?

Me: Veggie lasagna at lunch.

Nurse: Hmm. Great.

Me: It was OK.

Nurse: For dinner?

Me: Veggie lasagna… Leftover.

Nurse: Oh… Lasagna again.

Me: It was OK.

Nurse: Anything else?

Me: Sandwich bread…

Nurse: Plain?

Me: No, sandwich bread with cheese, tomato, pickles, ketchup, mustard, peanut butter, strawberry jam.

Nurse: Oh, my God! What else did you get?

Me: Pizza, cake and ice cream.

Nurse: Too much food. That's your problem.

Mom: What did you do, Sun? Are you crazy?

Dad: Where were we, Aura?

Mom: I think we were sleeping.

Me: It was the movie, guys!

Mom and Dad: Which movie?

Me: Oh, never mind.

Mom and Dad: Is Apple feeling bad, too?

Me: Yes, she is in the other room…

LOL

Yes, I promised I would never eat all there is in the fridge and in the freezer! Unless we are watching a terrifying movie!

July 29th
Friday

I'm feeling great now and so is Apple.

Our lovely family is going to the beach. We are going to camp.

I hate camping. I prefer a nice bed in a cozy hotel with a great view. Yes, we will have a great view, but we won't have a wonderful bed.

Dad forgot to punish me. LOL.

Mom reminded Dad to punish me. SNIFF.

August 1st
Monday

CRAZY NIGHT

Wow! I hate having a shower in a camping. My body was full of sand and I forgot to wash it off before using the soap. When Mom entered the shower, she screamed.

"Who left sand all over the soap?"

I was honest and told her it had been me. I had to leave the women's bathroom in a hurry to get soap for her in the tent. It was almost midnight and I thought nobody was up to face me wrapped in a towel. That was what I thought.

I met a stunning guy on my way to the tent. I panicked. My towel suddenly got stuck in a bush and I almost got naked in front of that top model (named Adam, LOL).

August 6th
Saturday

DEATH IN THE FAMILY

When we went camping, we left Bacon and Coffee with Uncle George and Aunt Myra. As soon as we came back, they called us to tell the bad news.

Bacon had been found dead.

They didn't know what had happened to our pet. He had been found lying in the backyard. Coffee was crying beside the body of his old fellow. Everybody started crying. Mom then decided to call a vet to know what had happened.

"This pig was thirteen years old. He died because he was an old pig."

We didn't know our pig's age. When we adopted him, he was a big pig, I guess.

After we cried a river, we decided to cremate Bacon. Mom, Dad, and Cosmo thought it was the best choice.

We had received a flyer from a company called Heaven Pet Crematory. It had been left in our post office box.

Mom called and the man came to take Bacon.

We wrapped Bacon in his favorite blanket. We decided to pray for him.

I started the prayer,

"Our beloved Bacon,

We love you and we will love you forever. You were our best friend ever.

We don't want to meet you soon. We would like to meet you in a hundred years. Please, wait for us.

Be happy with your new friends in heaven.

From dust you came, and to dust you shall return."

My parents stared at me while I was saying these words. Well, I have been in three burials, many services, and had learnt some words.

My brother also decided to say something.

"Rest in peace, dear friend. We will miss you."

If you think boys don't cry, you should have seen my brother Cosmo!

I started crying. I didn't want my pet turned into ashes.

We wrapped our Bacon in his favorite blanket.

Goodbye, Bacon. See you in Heaven, I thought.

We cried and hugged ourselves.

Nobody wanted to have dinner. We went to bed with our hearts in pain.

August 7th
Sunday

Dear diary,

My heart was broken into pieces. So I wrote this letter to Bacon and read it to my family.

Dear Bacon,

I woke up this morning and I didn't see you. I walked around the house looking for you. I went to the living room, to the bedrooms, to the kitchen, and to the backyard and didn't find you. Where's my cute pet?

Then I realized you aren't with us anymore. I saw your bed and I decided to sit beside it, so that I could stay a little longer beside you. I could feel your smell. I cried because I missed you. I finally slept. I dreamed about you.

You were in a wonderful place. The sky was of a wonderful blue I had never seen before and thousands of birds were flying above me. The grass you were on was of a light green which filled my heart. You were beautiful and funny too! You couldn't stop jumping, running up and down, and playing tricks to make me smile again. You wanted me to feel happy and you made it. I couldn't feel unhappy seeing you so happy!

> We jumped and rolled over the grass and we had so much fun that we had to take a little rest. We stayed together and then you told me how much that place was nice to you. You talked about your friends and told me there was no pain, sadness, or diseases around and that everybody was happy there.
> "Here's my Heaven" you said.
> Then you pointed at a beautiful hill. I'll be there waiting for you when it's time to be together again. Don't forget, even being far away from me, that I'll always be beside you. At the very moment, we will go down the hill and finally we will play together forever and ever in our Heaven.

Mom said it was a lovely and sad letter and started crying.
Dad sobbed. Cosmo dried some tears.
Coffee barked. He was sad too.
We had some soup for dinner and went to bed early.

August 12th
Friday

The man from Heaven came with Bacon's ashes. Bacon was very heavy.

It was kind of weird taking that blue box with Bacon inside it. Dad helped me put the ashes inside the house.

"Where?" we asked ourselves.

"Over the fireplace, until we have a nice place" Dad suggested.

As soon as Cosmo and Mom got home, we told them about Bacon's arrival.

We got sad again.

August 15th
Monday

Mass in memory of Bacon Smith.

I didn't know that everybody in school knew we had a pig as a pet. Many people came to comfort me last Friday. I was lying on bed when the bell rang. Bruno Myers was the first to get in. Then came Rick Cole, Adam Liang, Stewart "Rotten", Apple, Trip, Emily, Vicky, Monica, Sophia, Hanna, and Peaches, asking if we were going to do a mass service.

I told them my Bacon had already been cremated.

"Where are you going to put the ashes?" they asked.

"I don't know. They are actually on the fireplace, in a jar."

"What?"

That "what" impressed me more than my Bacon's ashes.

Some of my best friends agreed we needed a ceremony. Iago also agreed. So we decided to have this "service" on Sunday morning.

"After my Sunday School for Jewish studies" said one of them. "After my Baptist Sunday School" said another. "After the mass" said an another.

That's when I got to know everyone's religion.

"OK. After everybody's Sunday School, you can come over. And we will take Bacon to the woods where we used to play together."

Well, diary, I felt fine. I had many friends, they were concerned about my sadness and wanted to be with us at this sad time.

But on Sunday morning I woke up and woke up the rest of the family.

I told them I wasn't feeling glad to share that moment with everyone besides my family. And so we had breakfast, took Bacon in his jar, Coffee, and went to the woods.

When the people began to show up, we explained everything.

We had put Bacon's picture on the fireplace and spread some pictures of him on the dining table. Everybody wanted to look at him.

Mom made a carrot cake and Dad an orange juice. We shared the moment and I felt better.

I think they understood that it was a family moment. But I felt better having so many nice friends. Even Stewart "Rotten" was nice and cool!

August 20th
Saturday

Yes, my parents are detectives! They found me and Coffee hugging each other during our sleep. In fact, there were three of us on bed: Cosmo, me, and Coffee! We cried together and slept together.

"I think we can adopt another friend" said Cosmo.

"I think adopting another friend won't bring Bacon back to us. I want Bacon back" I answered him.

"But my heart says we need to help homeless friends" Cosmo continued.

"My heart is sad, Cosmo. No one will take Bacon's place."

"Tomorrow, after breakfast, we can go to the pet fair. We have to keep in mind that we can give another pet a home. And care."

"Well, I will go with you. But I will not adopt another pet. I have Coffee. Can we take Coffee with us?" I asked him.

He answered that it was a great idea.

August 21st
Sunday

No, it was not a good idea. Coffee didn't behave well.

PET ADOPTION FAIR
CLAYTON ANIMAL CARE CENTER
SUNDAY 21

10:00 AM to 4:00 PM
Free admission & giveaways
YOUR NEW BEST FRIEND IS
WAITING FOR YOU!

    As soon as Coffee entered the place, he started barking. He jumped on a place where baby cats were sleeping, scaring them a lot, tried to eat some birds, had a crush on a dog twice his size, and finally ate a hot dog someone was eating!
    When we were about to leave (or to be driven away!), my attention was caught by a dog with an eyepatch. He looked like a pirate.
    Coffee liked him. So did Cosmo. SO DID I!
    "Can we take him home?" we asked one of the people in charge.
    "Yes, but your parents have to sign this document saying they will protect him, care about him, give him the vaccines." We asked his name and laughed when the man told us: Sunny. Age: one.
    Healthy, castrated, and with only one eye. We didn't care. He seemed perfect for us!
    I couldn't believe I had changed my mind! My heart could fit a lovely adoptive dog! We went home quickly and asked our parents to come with us to the pet fair. Mom didn't want to, but Dad convinced her.
    And Sunny, age one, convinced them both!

August 25th
Thursday

"Where are my socks, Mom?"

In a minute I saw Sunny eating one of them! I panicked!

I grabbed the other one before he ate it. I gave him milk, water, waited for her to go to the backyard to do her business.

I called Cosmo and told him what had happened. Mom and Dad were working.

"Should we take him to the vet?"

"Let's wait a couple of hours."

We waited a couple of hours and nothing came out from Sunny.

We took him to the vet.

We explained to the vet, Mrs. Powell, what had happened.

She asked me to show her the size of the sock. I took the other sock out of my pocket and showed it to her.

"It's huge. The sock is not going to come out. We'll do an incision to take it out. Otherwise, it will go to the dog's intestine and that will be a problem!"

I called Cosmo aside and asked him how much money he had.

"Why?"

"We will have to pay for the surgery! It was our fault!"

"OURS?"

"Hummm… Yes. I was wearing the pair of socks, but they were YOURS!"

The vet didn't inform us the price. She said she had to do the surgery immediately. She would tell us the value after the surgery.

We then decided to call our parents. If something happened to our dog, we would feel guilty. In fact, I was feeling guilty. It was my fault!

We hugged our quiet dog and said goodbye. It could be our last hug! Sniff.

Cosmo took my hand and we decided to pray. Because we went to a lot of churches, we knew some of the prayers. We were still praying together when the vet left the surgery room. My parents entered the room right at that moment.

"What happened?" and blablabla.

"The dog is fine. Here's the sock." She gave us a plastic bag with a dirty sock inside.

"Sunny is very rowdy. You have to take care of him. He has been here many times, although he is only two years old. He was playing with a frog… You know, frogs fling a poison that can cause blindness. Sunny is so rowdy that his old owner donated him. He didn't instruct the dog.

Mom, Dad, and we were astonished.

"What are we going to do with Sunny?" they wanted to know.

"Instruct him!" we both answered.

August 27th
Saturday

The vet called us yesterday. Sunny was barking too loudly, had fell from the stretcher, and had swallowed a piece of string.

"I think he is all right now. Can you take Sunny home, please?"

Yes, we could.

We both also gave our money in order to pay the vet.

We completely ran out of money. We gave everything we had: bills, coins, coins, bills.

I am completely broke, diary. So is my lovely brother Cosmo.

August 29th
Monday

Sunny ate part of the fastener. I got crazy and mad at him! Adam told me to tell Sunny when he does something wrong, "It's ugly, very ugly!"

I did that a thousand times and then asked Cosmo to take care of him. I had to buy some clothing. I forgot I had no money. So I opened my closet and took an old T-shirt. Then I put it on Sunny. He looked funny in that T-shirt.

"Better behave!" I decided to keep him and Coffee by me.

Cosmo and I were hungry. Nothing special in the fridge, nothing special in the cabinet. Only a few eggs and lactose free milk in the fridge, brown sugar and oatmeal in the cabinet… And, on the fridge, three ripe bananas.

"A cake!" I remembered one of Mom's special cakes.

"Where's the recipe?" Cosmo wanted to know.

"Google?" I had no idea.

We decided: Google.

We blended the three eggs in the blender with the bananas. Then we added the two cups of oatmeal, the cup of brown sugar, a teaspoon of cinnamon and half cup of oil. Cosmo spread butter on a pan and then I put the dough. It smelt delicious!

Mom had taught us a few steps in the kitchen with oven, heat, temperature. So we baked the cake in the oven.

After thirty minutes, we took it out the oven! It smelt great, but it was flat as a cutting board!

"We forgot something! The baking powder!"

OMG! The baking powder! How could we be so stupid?

I have to tell you that in spite of forgetting the baking powder, the cake tasted great!

September 1st
Thursday

Adam came over yesterday. He wanted to start coaching Sunny. But Sunny still got his stitches. So he can't start coaching my dog. We sat on the sofa to watch a movie. We had popcorn, soda, and cake. Holidays are almost finished.

Dad came into the living room unexpectedly. He sat on the sofa with us, ate our popcorn and drank our soda. Coffee and Sunny were watching the movie with us. I bet he is jealous.

September 3rd

Saturday

We had to take Sunny to the vet. Time to remove the stitches!

Sunny didn't behave well. He tried to jump on the balcony full of toys and succeeded (he ate a fake dog cookie). We finally grabbed him (while Coffee watched us very quietly) and took him to the vet's room.

"Better keep an eye on this boy!" she advised us.

She removed the stitches and everything was OK.

"Goodbye, Sunny. I don't want you here anymore… Only for the vaccines!" she laughed.

Sunny waved his tail. We love him in spite of his bad manners!

Diary, did I tell you Coffee behaves like a dog now? Look at his tail… It's like Sunny's tail!

I wonder what he would do if we had a cat or a bird! LOL

I had to go to the market to buy some things Mom asked me. The list was not so long. I didn't see any delicacy. So I bought some onion rings (onions are vegetables, I am sure Mom will like it), popcorn (they are made of corn, she will like it too), chocolate, which is made of cocoa, which is a seed, and she likes seeds.

I hope she likes it.

September 4th

Sunday

Two more days before classes start!

I forgot I have to buy our next book: *Anne Frank's Diary*.

I went to the bookstore at the mall. Dad gave me money to buy the book. I met some friends there. We decided to have some ice cream. I had a triple with bananas and hot fudge on top. It was awesome.

When I got home, Cosmo asked to borrow my new book. "I have to read a book… any one. My English teacher told us to read any book." I panicked. I forgot to buy the book! I had the ice cream instead! Stupid creature! What am I going to say to my parents? That I ate the book? I need help!!!

September 5th
Monday

LABOR DAY

Time to stay in bed until late in the morning, late in the afternoon and until night. Mom has asked me to put the garbage away. I told her today is LABOR DAY!

"Labor Days is for commemorating people who work! Where do you work, lady?" she argued.

"I work at school every day" I answered.

"No, dear, you study every day. Dad and I work every day. That's the difference!"

"OK, I will take the litter away. By the way, who created Labor Day?" I wanted to know.

"Labor Day is celebrated on the first Monday of September. On this holiday, we are grateful for the contributions of the working class and how they help build America. Labor Day has been a national holiday since 1894 and is often celebrated with summer activities and the return of school."

"Now, time to work! I have laundry and you have the garbage!"

I had an idea! If I cleaned the neighbor's yard, I could earn some bucks. I have to buy a book and some make-up. And I have no money!

Great idea! Sun, you are a genius! Enjoy Labor Day… Working and earning money! Here I go, Mr. Brown! I hope I can buy the book, otherwise I'll be in trouble! Make--up, you've been left behind.

September 6th
Tuesday

Classes began today. I think I am allergic to school!
Coffee is allergic to school too. And so is Sunny.
Hey, what did you eat, fellows?
Mommmmmmmmm!

September 7th
Wednesday

I asked Dad to drop me at the bookstore. I needed to buy *Anne Frank's Diary*, the diary of a young girl.

Wow! A hard cover book cost US$12,39, the paperback one cost US$4,98. I checked on the Internet. An used one would be around US$0,10! I decided to take a look at the book inside the bookstore. I sat down and read the back.

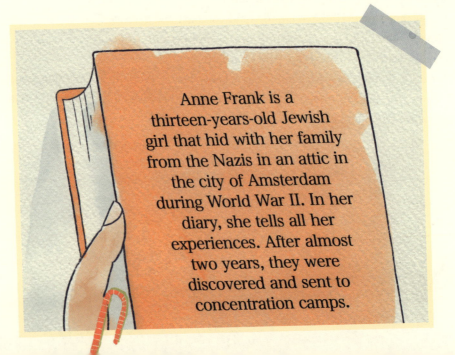

Anne Frank is a thirteen-years-old Jewish girl that hid with her family from the Nazis in an attic in the city of Amsterdam during World War II. In her diary, she tells all her experiences. After almost two years, they were discovered and sent to concentration camps.

Wow! I had to buy it immediately. It seemed to be very sad. I wished it had a happy end.

I took the paperback book, which was US$4,98, and went home, with my book and a backache!

September 13th
Tuesday

Our book test about *Anne Frank's Diary*. I'm not sure I got an A. I don't care if I succeeded. I loved this book. I don't know why teachers like to make so many questions. I think it is to prove that we have read the whole book.

One of the teacher's questions was "Who betrayed Anne Frank's family?". I answered that the betrayer was not found. It could be the neighbors, I suppose.

In our group, we discussed about why someone would do that. Apple said it was for food. We agreed. Food was difficult to get, so if anyone betrayed a Jew, he or she would have a reward.

The second question was easy. She asked why it was so dangerous for everyone when Anne screamed in her sleep. I answered that any noise heard from the annex put everyone's lives in danger. Anne's screaming might alert the wrong person to their presence.

The third question was easy. But we had to open the book and rewrite a part of it. She asked, "What does Anne want to become when the war is over?"

I knew she wanted to be a journalist. I myself want to be a journalist.

> "I must work, so as not to be a fool, to get on, to become a journalist, because that's what I want!... I can't imagine that I would have to lead the same sort of life as Mummy... and all the women who do their work and are then forgotten. I must have something besides a husband and children, something that I can devote myself to!"

September 16th
Friday

New Math exercises. I really don't know how to handle Maths. OMG!
Let's go to History.

CIVIL WAR

The American Civil War lasted from 1860 to 1865. It was fought between the northern and the southern states. The southern states didn't want the northern ones saying what they had to do. So, they decided to separate from them, forming what they called the Confederacy. The North wanted all the states to stay as one country, so they began to fight. More than 600,000 men on both sides died. The South was devastated. General Lee surrendered to General Grant on April 9, 1865 and the war was over.

We are planning to do a theatre about Civil War. Everything I know is in *Gone with the wind*, a very, very, very old movie. Every time I get a bad grade, I remember one of the movie's best quotes: "After all, tomorrow is another day!" LOL

September 18th
Sunday

Adam came over. He asked me to go out for an ice cream.
Mom said YES, Dad said NO.
"Ask Cosmo to go with you."
"Cosmo went out with Peaches!"
"You are too young to have a boyfriend!"
"We are not going to get married!"
"Take someone with you!"

"Sunny and Coffee?"

"Hummm…"

"You said 'someone'."

"I intended people!"

"They are family!"

"Okey dokey."

I regretted it. Sunny ate Adam's ice cream and Coffee someone else's.
Remember my change? I spent half of it with ice cream for two kids!

September 30th

Friday

Cosmo and Peaches broke up. Sorry for that. I really like Peaches. I don't know what in heaven's name she saw in my brother. He has a crush on Rebbecca, the most stupid girl in school!

I talked to Peaches on the phone this afternoon.

"What happened, Peaches?"

"I don't know, Sun. I think he doesn't like me anymore". SNIFF.

"How come?"

"He is too young to go steady with me."

"What?"

"I don't want to go steady with anybody. I just want someone faithful. And your brother is not. He is also going out with Rebbecca." Sniff.

Gosh! I couldn't imagine my brother could have two girlfriends. It is insane!

I went to his bedroom, knocked on the door. He was on the phone with Rebbecca. I asked to talk to him in private. I know that I am too young to talk about relationships. I haven't kissed yet, I have a single crush, but we learned with our parents about being faithful, about loyalty.

"You are wrong. If you didn't like Peaches anymore, you should have broken up with her. You are very wrong, brother."

He seemed ashamed. He told me he would apologize for his mistake.

Hope so!

"But I like Rebbecca. I am in love with her!"

Boys!

October 1st
Saturday

Watching TV with our friends "Steward Cute", Adam Liang, Apple, Emily, Vicky, Cosmo and Rebbecca (argh!). We are having popcorn and fruit juice. The movie is about an ET invasion.

Adam grabbed my hand during the movie. He said he was feeling awkward and scared. When Dad came in to bring us more popcorn, he saw us and said, "What's going on here?"

"I'm scared, Mr. Gomez. I'm feeling bad. Sun is trying to calm me down."

"Would you let go of her hand?" Dad asked him.

"Yes, sir…" and Adam threw up inside the popcorn bucket.

We were shocked. It was kind of funny, everybody running and trying to get away from that bad smell.

Mom heard the noise and came to see what was happening. She then helped Dad clean the mess and phoned my friend's parents.

They soon came over to my house and picked Adam up. It might be a virus.

Poor friend. Or boyfriend! LOL

October 3rd
Monday

Late at night.

Adam spent the weekend at the hospital. I think he is the big love of my live.

When I told Mom about my big love, she said, "Your dad was my first big love, honey! I am glad Adam is your big love, too. Let's have dinner".

I don't like it when Mom changes subjects. I was telling her about the love of my life and she says it is time to have dinner.

What do we do when we are in love, diary? My heart feels like it is jumping around when Adam looks at me. I can't go on living that way.

I will have a heart attack the day he kisses me. But he'd better be well soon. I don't want to be sick.

Well, diary, this is so cute! Our friends at school sent him notes of "good recovery".

October 5th
Wednesday

Adam Liang is back. He is better now. He is very thin and I think he is much thinner now.

Besides the project, we will have a test about the book we are reading, *Around the world in 80 days*. I am trying to help him. He hasn't read it and he won't have enough time to do it.

So he is at my house now, holding my hand to feel better while I explain the whole story to him.

"Are you sick again?" Cosmo asked Adam as soon he entered the living room.

I was as red as a tomato.

I hate my brother.

October 8th
Saturday

I heard Mom and Dad saying Aunt Myra and Uncle George are going to divorce! That's so unfair! Poor Iago! Who is he going to live with?

Hope not here!

October 10th
Monday

COLUMBUS DAY
(second Monday in October)

Another project to do. Columbus Day.

I asked myself who Christopher Columbus was. I had to read about him!

He was an Italian explorer, navigator, and colonizer. He was born in Genoa, Italy. He is often said as the discoverer of the New World. I read that there is evidence that the first Europeans to sail across the Atlantic were Viking explorers from Scandinavia. Our land was already populated by indigenous peoples, who had discovered the Americas thousands of years before.

Columbus Day originated as a celebration of Italian-American heritage and was first held in San Francisco in 1869.

So, it is a bit of a confusing date, I think.

I can't understand the parades going on in the country… And I have classes!

Columbus, this is not fair!

October 14th
Friday

We had pasta at the cafeteria. I think I've been having pasta since I was born.

Pasta with zucchini, pasta with asparagus, pasta with tomato sauce, pasta with cauliflower, pasta with garlic, pasta with peas, four cheese, with pumpkin, pesto, buttermilk squash, with roasted vegetables, with broccoli.

I felt nausea. I was itching. My face got red and so did my body.

I went to the nursery. I felt sick.

Dad picked me up at school.

"I think you are sick."

I was pretty sure.

October 15th
Saturday

It was so nice staying in bed, having Mom by my side. She thinks I have intolerance to gluten.

"Grandpa Mario was also intolerant to gluten. Maybe you are like him!"

"What am I going to eat? Anything at all?" I panicked.

"Well, let's see a doctor!" Mom decided to make me a gluten free sandwich.

OMG!

October 18th
Tuesday

After the doctor's visit…

"She must eat protein. It can be soy, fish, meat, nuts… She is allergic to gluten. That's not a problem!"

"Not a problem? I've heard gluten is everywhere! What am I going to eat?"

Dear diary, this news came as a tsunami for me. My vegetarian parents were pale, desperate, had a long conversation… And decided to change a little. We can have fish from now on.

That's a problem! I don't like fish either!

Well, they went to the supermarket and came back with the trunk of the car full of GLUTEN-FREE STUFF.

Disgusting. I think they are disgusting!

October 21st
Friday

I feel much better. I'm having gluten-free lunch at the cafeteria.
I sit with my gluten-free friends (we are eleven!), so we can discuss about our allergy.
"My stomach hurts."
"I went to the hospital twice this year."
"There is a new store on Fifth Avenue…"
"There is a new website with wonderful new recipes…"
I am fed up with this subject.
Adam came by and tried to cheer me up.
He is my boyfriend and my best friend ever!

October 23rd
Sunday

Great news: Uncle George and Aunt Myra are not getting a divorce anymore!

Nice news: they are going to Maui for a second honeymoon.

Bad news: Iago is here! In my bedroom!!! For ten days!!!

October 24th
Monday

Iago is a sleepwalker. He woke up this morning, walked to the kitchen, had all gluten-free ice cream he could, opened the backyard door and came back to bed. He left the door of the fridge open and Sunny and Coffee had lots of fun!

When Mom woke up this morning, she yelled. Everything was on the floor. They left the lettuce, the broccoli, the tomatoes… And they ate my gluten-free bread, ice cream, leftover pasta.

Look at the mess:

October 29th
Saturday

My parents decided to take us to the mall. There is a new restaurant there.

It was kind of funny. Rebbecca's parents were sitting at the next table and Peaches' family was on the other side. This is a small town and this is a new restaurant.

Cosmo was white as a sheet of paper. Iago didn't stop talking, thank God!

Mom and Dad looked at the menu, looking for something everybody could eat.

They thought about many fish possibilities and finally went back to the vegetarian options. LOL!

Mom's choice: vegetarian fish (imitation fish made from yam).

Dad's choice: vegetarian Singapore-style fried vermicelli (which I think looks like worms).

Iago's: top sirloin with Caesar salad.

Cosmo's: quinoa burger and cheddar cheese.

Mine: salmon with gluten-free cheddar cheese.

The food was awesome.

Our desserts were: cream caramel, *crème brûlée*, passion fruit mousse, vanilla ice cream with hot banana, and, for me, raspberry sorbet.

When we asked for the bill, Dad almost had a heart attack. It was huge!

"Well, we don't do that every day, honey."

"I don't want to live with my parents anymore. You are so much better!" Iago said.

I'm really worried about this, diary. We want him to go back home!

October 31st
Monday

HALLOWEEN

7:00 p.m.

Iago is great. He helped me make many fake wounds on my body.

I looked like a zombie. He dressed like a ghost with one of my mom's old sheets.

Cosmo is dressed like a mummy and so are the dogs. So funny.

Iago is so creative. I loved my costume!

10:00 p.m.

We went to the neighborhood for "trick-or-treating". We got a lot of candies, chocolate bars, and sweets.

We met Apple and Peaches as Snow White and Sleeping Beauty. Rebecca was dressed as herself, a silly costume... LOL!

Adam was dressed as a mummy. Creepy!

11:00 p.m.

Mr. Brown's wife opened her front door and had a heart attack when she saw me with my fake wounds.

She fell on the floor and we started screaming. We thought she was playing with us. She wasn't!

I explained to her husband, Mr. Brown, that my injuries were fake, but he was so mad!

We helped him put her on the sofa, went to the kitchen and got some water.

My body was really scary!

He didn't give us treats and we left his house without tricking!

Midnight

Our team was the best. People were scared, got frightened, gave us everything... Even a peanut butter bottle!

Our costumes were the most amazing ones!

Iago is awesome!

November 2nd
Wednesday

My wonderful cousin is back in his home. Sniff.

I think he is a nice cousin. Hope my aunt and uncle are still married.

November 3rd
Thursday

It's snowing a lot.

I need new clothes. I hate it when Mom buys clothing at Donation For Life.

It's a store (and yes, they have a website!!!) where you can help poor children around the world. When someone shops there, a school gets desks, a poor child gets some food. I know it's good helping people abroad, I know a little lift from us is often all people need to transform their communities forever… But I want new clothes! Everyone at school thinks I am from another planet!

There is a new store at the mall. It is called New Century and all my friends have clothes from that store.

MOM!!! Help me to be normal!

November 6th
Sunday

I went to the movies with Adam Liang, Cosmo and his girlfriend, Apple, Trip, and Emily.

It was a comedy and I wore my new clothes that I bought yesterday.

"You are pretty!" said Adam.

"You are handsome!" I replied.

But really, diary, his clothes seemed the ones I used to wear.

Maybe his mother is fond of Donation For Life.

We bought popcorn and soda. After ten minutes of movie, he grabbed my hand.

My heart was bumping and jumping. I really like him!

Can I tell you something? My brother was kissing his silly girlfriend. It was a noisy kiss. When Adam kisses me in the mouth, I will ask him not to make much noise. Silence is gold, as Dad says.

November 8th
Tuesday

Wow, diary! No classes today.

Election Day.

We will have a report about Republicans and Democrats.

My mom's family is Democrat. By the other hand, my dad's family is Republican. I know Republicans believe that each person is responsible for her own place in society. Government should enable each person to secure the benefits of society for themselves, their families, and for those who are unable to care for themselves.

I don't know much about Democrats. I asked Dad and he explained that Democrats believe it is the responsibility of the government to care for all individuals, even if it means giving up some individual rights.

"Which one is better?"

"I would say Republican" Dad said, "but we have had many nice Democrats, such as Kennedy, Jimmy Carter, Bill Clinton. The delegates we vote for support the particular person they want to run for president. By voting, you are making your voice heard and registering your opinion on how you think the government should act."

I liked most that "Democrats believe it is the responsibility of the government to care for all individuals, even if it means giving up some individual rights."

I asked Dad if I can be a Democrat someday and he answered, "Yes, you can. This is called freedom."

But I didn't like his smile. It was scary!

Mom's candidate is Alberta Dickson; Dad's candidate is Paul Johnson.

I hope Alberta Dickson wins. We have never had a woman for President in the USA.

November 11th
Friday

Our Geography teacher was very mad. He said NO for copying and pasting from Wikipedia.

"You were supposed to write your report. I want you to do it by your own."

And he gave us our reports back. Mine was copied from Wikipedia, too. I felt so embarrassed. It was a report about Earth's features, resources, and climates. It was not so difficult, but I was in a hurry and decided to copy and paste. She found out! Shame on you, Sun! I won't ever do it again!

That's incredible! In the VETERANS DAY!

Do you know what a Veterans Day is? I am a veteran at Wikipedia! But it didn't work. No more Wikipedia!

There's a Vietnam veteran who stays every single day in front of Marcy's Grocery.
He is homeless. Some say he got crazy, but I don't think so. He seems to be very funny. He tells jokes, sings, and plays a guitar. He also asks for money. He says the government took everything he had: his dignity and his left leg.
Poor man!

VETERANS DAY

Veterans Day is an official United States holiday that honors people who have served in the U.S. Armed Forces, also known as veterans. It is a federal holiday that is commemorated on November 11. Veterans Day celebrates the service of all U.S. military veterans, while Memorial Day is a day of remembering the men and women who died while serving.

November 18th
Friday

Mom and Dad went to the movies. Cosmo and I decided to make some pasta with marinara sauce.
I cut my finger, he cut his finger, we made a big mess, but the pasta was awesome!

Here's the recipe:

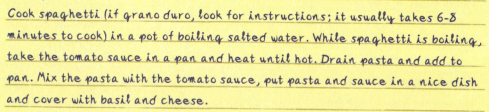

<u>You will need:</u>
- 1 pound spaghetti
- 2 cups ready tomato sauce
- 2/3 cup grated cheese
- a handful of basil

<u>Preparation</u>
Cook spaghetti (if grano duro, look for instructions; it usually takes 6-8 minutes to cook) in a pot of boiling salted water. While spaghetti is boiling, take the tomato sauce in a pan and heat until hot. Drain pasta and add to pan. Mix the pasta with the tomato sauce, put pasta and sauce in a nice dish and cover with basil and cheese.

We cut our fingers grating the cheese. But it was worth it!

November 24th
Thursday

THANKSGIVING

During the 17th century, when the King controlled the Church of England, some people decided to escape from the King's rules. So, around one hundred people left England, sailing on a ship. Those people, called Pilgrims, landed in Plymouth after a six-week journey. It was on December 11, 1620. The weather was cold and the land was strange. Luckily, native Americans helped them bringing seeds, food, and teaching them how to survive in this new land.

The Pilgrims planted those seeds and plants and succeeded. They celebrated the good fortune with a Thanksgiving party. They cooked turkey, duck, fish, pumpkins, sweet potatoes, corn, and cranberries. The native Americans who had helped them so much during their first year were invited to the party and they shared a good day of Thanksgiving. This harvest feast in 1621 is called the "First Thanksgiving". So Thanksgiving became an important tradition in the United States. It is a day of giving thanks for all that we have.

We will have turkey for Thanksgiving! That's awesome for a vegetarian family!
Great-grandmother Sally and Grandma Sophie will come with the turkey.
Grandpa Philip died when I was a baby. The two women live together in Charlottesville, fifty miles away.
Mom's parents died in a car accident when she was twelve. She was raised by a Mexican aunt who lives in Guadalajara now. She has only a sister, Aunt Myra.
We will also have gravy for the turkey.
I'm so glad our family will be here! Mom's brother, Uncle George, will come too. His second wife is Aunt Emily and we like her more than the first one, ex-Aunt Olivia, who lives in Canada now with my two twin cousins, Oscar and David.

November 25th
Friday

My BirthDay

Twelve! I can't believe I am twelve years old!
Dad, Mom, Cosmo and the dogs came in my bedroom before breakfast. They sang "Happy Birthday" to me, as always. I was still sleeping. I like it when my family does that. They've done it since I was a little girl.
"We are going to have dinner tonight" they promised.
Nice.
Dad went to school to pick me up. Cosmo went home by bus.
"I have some things to do downtown. We are going to buy you a birthday cake, OK?"

"OK."

When we got home, almost two hours later, I was so so hungry, I opened the door of the car and went right to the kitchen.

"SURPRISE!"

Diary, I almost had a heart attack, like Grandma says. All my school friends were here! They prepared me a surprise party, with popcorn, hot dogs, soda, balloons!

Everybody was here! All my friends and my super friend Adam, who gave me a cute card and gluten-free chocolate, so sweet!

We had all hot dogs we could have, lots of soda, lots of cake. Yes, the hot dogs were gluten-free and the sausages were made of soy. About the cake… Absolutely normal! OMG! I had a thin slice!

We also listened to music and Cosmo, believe it or not, was so cool!

Thanks, Mom, thanks, Dad, thanks everybody!

December 3rd
Saturday

Mom is not feeling well today. Maybe she has got the flu.

Dad woke up, went to the beauty parlor and told Audrey, the girl who works with Mom, that she wouldn't work for a couple of days.

Then he came back home and made the nicest breakfast for everybody in ages! Waffles with syrup, milk, corn flakes, scrambled eggs, toast, and jam!

We put many things on a tray and took it to Mom upstairs. She loved it!

"I think I will have the flu every month!"

After the breakfast, Dad went to his office to work on a new star he has just discovered.

"Its name will be AURA" he smiled at me.

December 4th
Sunday

Mom is a little better.

She laughed a lot when Dad took Coffee and Sunny to their bedroom. Sunny had a flower in his mouth and Coffee a balloon, on which Dad had written a note:

"Get better, honey!"

It is snowing outside. We left school and decided to make a snowman. Cosmo is now dating Peaches again. I feel happy because I like her. She is my best friend's sister.

Adam, Apple, Vicky, and Monica came too.

We were already working on our snowman, when Ricky Cole, Stewart "Rotten", Bruno Myers, and Sophia came, too.

We started a snow ball fight and it was pretty funny.

Apple told me she has a crush on Stewart "Rotten". I can't believe that. He is a bad person. I don't like him.

Look how funny our snow ball fight was!

December 8th
Thursday

There is a new kid in our classroom. His name is T. J. (Thomas Jacob Taylor).

Apple and I noticed T. J. doesn't have a backpack. We asked him why he comes to school with a travel bag. It is so weird. The travel bag is enormous!

"I asked my dad money to buy a backpack. But when I passed in front a pet shop, I spent the money in an aquarium. When I asked more money to my dad, he said I would have to be creative to carry my books to school. He had ran out of money. So, the only way to carry my books from home to school is this… In my travel bag!"

Adam was sorry for him. So was the whole classroom.

On the way back home, in the school bus, I told Cosmo about it. He reminded me he had a backpack when he was in kindergarten. We could give it to T. J.

December 10th
Saturday

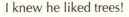

Mom is so much better. But she went to see a doctor last afternoon.

Diary, it was kind of funny last morning. We went to school with the bear backpack. When we got there, many of my friends had had the same idea. Sophia brought her blue sparkling backpack, Hanna brought her princess backpack, Ricky Cole, his superhero backpack, Emily, her favorite backpack since she was four, Anna, her ladybug backpack, Vicky, a duck backpack, Monica, a zebra backpack, Apple, an apple backpack, Adam Liang, a shark backpack, Bruno Myers, his frog backpack, Stewart "Rotten" his best ever dinosaur backpack.

I found in my closet a tree backpack. We used it to go camping.

He was so happy with our care. AND CHOSE MINE TO BE HIS BACKPACK.

I knew he liked trees!

He is a nice kid!

December 14th
Wednesday

I got a C in Math. Dad is going to kill me!
I got a C- in History. Mom is going to kill me!
I got a C in English, which is my best subject. What is going on with me???
I don't like me anymore!

December 16th
Friday

How am I going to tell my parents about my grades? I have never had those bad grades before.

"Hope they don't mind much about my D+ in EVERYTHING!" said my brother Cosmo.

"What are we going to do?"

"Hide it?"

"Tell them during supper?"

"Hide it."

December 18th
Sunday

"Mom and I have an important announcement…" Dad was feeling embarrassed.

"Yes, in fact, I do… I hope we can survive to something that is happening in this family."

THEY KNEW IT! OUR GRADES!

"You know, you know…" I started.

Coffee and Sunny barked at mom. They have been barking a lot to her, I don't know why.

"Did you open the envelope?" Dad asked us.

The grades! They came in an envelope! Stupid Cosmo might have forgotten the envelope on his bed!

"Yes! But we were not going to sign it!" Cosmo tried to explain.

"What's going on with this family? Can't we have a secret?" Dad was pretty mad at us.

"We don't have a secret anymore" replied Cosmo.

"Are you mad at us? I promise I will study harder" I said.

"Oh, we have a problem here…" Mom smiled. "Are you talking about grades? Your grades?"

"Yes."

"Yes, Mom."

"I am talking about my blood exams. I have leukemia. I hope you know what it is."

"What?" We were astonished.

Then, while Mom looked at our dogs, that didn't stop barking, Dad explained she was sick. But she would start a treatment in two or three days.

"Are you going to have a haircut like those we watch on TV?" We wanted to know.

"Yes!" Dad said.

"No!" Mom said.

I looked at our dogs. They were not barking anymore!

Mom started crying and Dad held her. Cosmo and I left the room.

I went to my bedroom, threw myself on my bed and cried a river. I loved my Mom and would never let her go. I had already heard stories about people who died of cancer, who died of leukemia. What could I do for my mother? Pray!

I closed my eyes and talked to God.

"God, can you hear me? I know I am just a kid, but please, don't take our mother from us. We need her. You don't need her now, I suppose. She is more important for us at the moment. Don't let her suffer, I beg you."

Then I said "amen", because I have heard my friends saying "amen" many times. I think it is important when you talk to God. It is a kind of deal.

Cosmo entered my bedroom to talk about Mom. I told him I was praying. He asked me to tell him how to do it. I told him it was a sincere talk, that was all.

"How can I do it?" he asked.

"Close your eyes and talk to God. Easy. You will feel better."

He did it. It was a long prayer.

After his prayer, we talked about Mom.

"What can we do to help her?" I asked him.

"Be at her side, be loving, helpful…"

"Let's start doing that!" I suggested.

We went back to the living room. My Dad was still comforting Mom. We hugged her and told her we loved her and would stay by her side all the time.

"I love you guys. I feel much better now. In fact, I feel great!"

She smiled and gave us a bear hug.

December 19th
Monday

T. J. comes to school every day with his tree backpack. I bet his mom buys his clothes at the same store our mom does. He was crying during lunch. I asked him why.

"My mom wants to move to another city! AGAIN!"

I told him I had an idea. Hanna always comes to school with her cell phone, which is not allowed, but she does it anyway. I called my group and told them T. J. didn't want to leave us. Then we wrote a big poster: "T. J., please, stay with us. We love you!" And we sent it to his mom's cell phone.

That would work.

…

Let's decorate our Christmas tree!

Dad brought a real pine tree (he had planted tree seedlings before he brought this one home) and we started decorating it. Mom didn't want to join us. She hasn't been in a good mood lately. Our tree is wonderful.

December 21st

Wednesday

Mom's leukemia is on stage 1.

She was not feeling well yesterday, had stayed on bed for a couple of days and decided to go to the doctor again. We were worried about her all day long. During dinner, she smiled at us and said she is going to start the treatment!

I feel so sad, diary.

My brother Cosmo left dinner and went to his bedroom. I think Coffee and Sunny noticed it, for they put their paws on their noses and stayed there lying on the floor, with sad eyes.

"The doctor said I am going to be OK. I will have a treatment, I have to stop working for now…" she explained.

"I know everything is going to be fine, Mom. You will do great!"

"Thanks, family. You are so supportive!" she thanked us.

I went back to my bedroom. I had a lot of stuff to do, but could do nothing.

December 22nd

Thursday

I told Apple about Mom. She knew it. Cosmo had already told Peaches.

"I'm thinking about having a haircut, like those scenes we see on TV. When people have cancer, you know. I think my mom would like it."

"Is she going to die?"

"No! There are lots of treatments for leukemia nowadays!"

"Can I have a haircut too?"

"Sure!"

I thought Apple was so nice for doing that for my mom.

"When can we go to the salon?"

"Tomorrow Audrey will be there. Don't tell anyone!"

"I won't."

"Promise?"

"Promise."
"We are not going to take the bus."
"Done."
...
I looked at myself in the mirror. Goodbye hair, you are the best part of me.

December 23rd
Friday

When we got to the salon, we were shocked. Cosmo, Peaches, and the whole gang were there. Girls talk too much. Boys do the same, I guess.

Audrey had already done her hair… to zero.

"Does your mother know you are going to do it?"

"It is a surprise!"

"I might get fired for that."

Cosmo was the first.

I was the second.

Apple, the third, and Peaches, the fourth. And then came Adam, Rick Cole, Stewart cute "Rotten", Rebecca, Bruno Myers, Emily, Vicky, Monica, Sophia, Hanna, T. J. and his tree backpack.

Each one of us had a different haircut.

We were quiet. Extremely quiet.

We took a bus to go home. Audrey went with us. Everybody in the bus was staring at us. "Gang of nuts", they were probably be thinking.

When we entered the living room, Dad got pale. When Mom saw us, she hugged one by one. She could not stop saying, "You are the love of my life."

"I'll be fine. I promise you all."

Sunny and Coffee barked at us. They seemed happy.

December 25th
Sunday

Christmas' Eve

Dear diary,

I think I am the happiest girl in the world.

I have to tell you: Mom phoned up each family, saying she hasn't asked my friends to have a haircut. She also apologized for her helper, Audrey. The families were upset, but understood the feeling of each of us. Friendship. That is all.

We know Mom will be fine. She is fine.

I haven't asked for anything for Christmas. But I can't deny I haven't seen my parents putting some packages under the Christmas tree.

CHRISTMAS

I woke up early in the morning. Cosmo, me, and the dogs went to our parents' bedroom.

"MERRY CHRISTMAS, EVERYBODY!" we shouted.

Coffee and Sunny had Christmas hats on their heads. I had a bell and Cosmo a bag with our presents inside it.

We made a big noise and the dogs, in a minute, were on my parents' bed.

We had bought Mom a scarf and Dad a pair of wool socks, for Sunny had eaten his last pair of socks.

"Do you know what I like

most in this family?" Dad asked us.

"Tell us!" smiled Mom.

"The nice way we can hold life and its unrespectable way."

That was true!

We jumped on their bed and gave them a bear hug.

For the first time, diary, I really didn't care about my Christmas presents, if they were from New Century or from Donation For Life.

Family was the best present I could ever have!

December 30th
Friday

During lunch.

"Mom, when are you going to get a haircut?" Cosmo and I wanted to know.

"Well, I don't think I am going to have one... The doctor said nothing about it!"

"I can't believe we had a haircut for nothing... I mean..." I am always saying stupid things.

In the afternoon.

Mom had a haircut. She has no hair now, like us (but she doesn't have a Mohican hairdo).

I wanted to know why she did that if she was not supposed to lose hair.

"Well, we are family, you know, and if my kids and their friends are like this, I am going be the same."

Dad entered the living room with the same Mohican hairdo we had.

This is my family.

Crazy and lovely people I really care about.

December 31st
Saturday

Cosmo and Peaches are fine. I think he is going to be faithful from now on. We have had two or three talks about that. Dad also talked to him two weeks ago. So did Mom. And so did the whole world. LOL. He deserved all those talks.

Adam is here, by my side. All my friends are here, too. We look pretty weird with all these hairdos. Some of my friends decided to dye them (using the colors of the USA and Mexico flags).

Adam wants to read you, diary, but I am not going to let him do it.

There are some things only a girl and her best best friend and confidant should know. Am I right?

Happy New Year, diary. Happy New Year, family. Happy New Year, Sun! Happy New Year, Coffee and Sunny.

Happy New Year, Adam Liang!

I hope I have a great new year, with all my friends around me, with my dogs, my mom and dad, my bother Cosmo, who sometimes bothers me, but hey, he is OK, after all!

I want neither a new cell phone, nor a new tablet, nor fancy boots. I just want a healthy family, my friends, and my school. Yes, I love school. Sometimes I wish it could be closed for refurnishing… But on the next day I forget these feelings completely and I think learning makes me feel better to understand the world.

Telma Guimarães

Hello! My name is Telma Guimarães. I had many diaries when I was a teenager. At the age of eighteen, I went to the United States to study in a high school as an exchange student. I lived in Conyers, a town in the state of Georgia. My father was the Principal of one school in my hometown (Marilia, São Paulo), and coincidently Mr. Jerry Rochelle, my "American father", was the principal of Newton County High School, where I took the senior grade. It was so nice! I learned a lot with him. My American mother, Sandy Powell also taught me a lot about Civil War. My brother Eric and sister Karen were so cool with me. We shared so many wonderful stories together. I always wanted to be an English teacher. So I taught English during twenty-one years. I had already published more than forty books at that time and I realized I couldn't do both. I decided to quit teaching and it was very painful. After four years of hard work I published my first book for teens. And I didn't stop anymore. I have published more than one hundred and seventy books for children, teens, in Portuguese, English and Spanish. Have fun with SUN'S DIARY!

Rômolo

I was born in Foz do Iguaçu, state of Paraná, in 1983 and I am graduated in graphic design. Currently I collaborate as an illustrator for various publishers, newspapers and advertising agencies. Some of my work has been recognized and rewarded by the Folha de S. Paulo and the Animamundi Festival. As an artist, I took part in several group exhibitions in Brazil and other countries. I am the author of the comics *Malditos designers*, published by the Gato Preto publishing house, in 2014.

Este livro foi produzido para a Editora do Brasil em abril de 2016.